Painting out the Stars

MAL PEET & ELSPETH GRAHAM

ILLUSTRATED BY

MICHAEL FOREMAN

WALKER
BOOKS

First published as *Painting Out the Stars* in 2011 by Walker Books Ltd
87 Vauxhall Walk, London SE11 5HJ

"Cloud Tea Monkeys" first published in picture book form
in 1999 and republished in 2010

2 4 6 8 10 9 7 5 3 1

Text © 1999, 2010, 2011 Mal Peet and Elspeth Graham
Illustrations © 2011 Michael Foreman

This book has been typeset in ITC Veljovic

Printed and bound in Great Britain by Clays Ltd, St Ives plc

British Library Cataloguing in Publication Data:
a catalogue record for this book is available from the British Library

ISBN 978-1-4063-2486-0

www.walker.co.uk

For Rhys, Harry and Hugh

Contents

The Mysterious Traveller

There were five riders but six camels, travelling fast. Desperately fast. They were being chased, hunted. But because of the fading light and the dust thrown up by the camels' feet, they could not tell how close their pursuers were.

The camel without a rider was called Jin-Jin. He was fierce and quick-tempered and very intelligent, which was why he carried the travellers' most precious item. It was hidden in a woven basket, and Jin-Jin carried it as carefully as he could.

The riders were slithering down into a low and rocky valley when Jin-Jin sensed the danger. The danger that was far greater than the men following them. His clever nostrils read it in the air, and he roared a warning, digging his huge feet into the ground. The rider leading him turned in his saddle and swore angrily.

"On, Jin-Jin! On! On!" Then his face changed, because he saw what Jin-Jin had read on the wind. Behind them, where

moments before the evening sky had been, there was now a boiling wall of sand and dust like a tidal wave.

A desert storm.

There was no time to find shelter. The storm hurtled into the valley and struck the travellers like an enormous fist, blinding them. The howling, whirling brown air blotted out the sun and the rocks and everything except itself.

The riders and their camels vanished into it.

* * *

Issa, as usual, left his house before dawn and went to watch the sun being born again. At first it was a tiny red glimpse, as if someone had lit a fire among the distant hills. Slowly at first, then more quickly, it grew and swelled until it floated above the hills like a fat, shivery bubble. The colours of the desert came alive.

Issa's old eyes had watched thousands of dawns, but still it seemed to him that each one was a miracle. It lifted his heart. On this particular morning, however, the bottom edge of the sun was not as bright as normal. Blurry. Veiled. Issa squinted at it, then took a deep breath of the cold desert wind, testing its smell with his nose.

"Mmm," he murmured to himself. "Yes. Something has changed. There has been a storm in the hills, I think."

He turned to go back to his house. It was time for his prayers. Then he stopped.

A flash of bright colour had tickled his eye.
A scrap of cloth fluttering from the thorn
fence of his goat pen. He plucked it free
and studied it. A ribbon of some sort, richly
embroidered in black and green and red,
with two golden threads running through it.

Issa knew it had not been made by one
of his own people. The pattern told him this.
This ribbon had travelled a long way. And it
was not the kind of thing that anyone would
lose or throw away. Issa gazed at the hills for
a long moment, thinking. Then he hurried
to his house. He said his prayers. He filled
a goatskin flask with water and wrapped
a flatbread in a cloth. Then he fetched his
donkey from her stable.

"Are you in a good mood today, Donkey?
Yes? Good, because we have work to do."

Then the old man climbed onto her back
and together they headed out towards the
sun.

* * *

Issa was a guide. No, not a guide. The guide.
He knew the desert better than any other
human being. He knew its tracks and its
tricks. He knew its moods and its mountains.

14

In daylight he could read its colours, its breezes, its shadows. His eyes saw signs where other eyes saw only blank emptiness. At night he could read the map of the stars and the scents threaded on the air. And perhaps because he loved the desert, he was never lost in it.

When someone died, people would say, "He has gone where Issa cannot find him."

Because of his knowledge, because he had magic in his eyes, Issa was an important man. Travellers sought him out. They paid him handsomely to lead them safely through the shifting desert's dangers. And there were many travellers who passed through Issa's small town, most of them traders. They came from the north, their caravans – long lines of camels and donkeys – laden with salt. They came from the south, their caravans laden with gold. The dusty roads they all travelled met in Issa's town.

The traders would ask, "Who can guide us through the maze of hills to the east?" Or, "Who knows where there is water between here and the Great Lake?"

"Issa," people would say. "You need Issa. His house is that way. Look for the crooked gate."

But on the day that changed his life, Issa and his donkey were alone beneath the hot gaze of the sun.

"Stop, Donkey," Issa said, tapping the animal's neck. "Let us stop and think."

They had been travelling for several hours and had come to the low wall of the hills. The ways in had been hidden by the storm. Issa stared, working out how the world had become different. Then the donkey's ears twitched.

"What?" Issa said.

The donkey's ears twitched again, and this time Issa heard something that sounded like a human cough, or groan.

"Good girl," he said. "Come on. Take me there."

They struggled into a shallow valley. He had been here before, but its shape had been changed by disaster.

The donkey stopped again. Another harsh cry, louder and closer now. Where the grey rock wall of the valley rose out of the sand, something moved.

Squinting, Issa made out the neck and head, the shoulders and hump, of a camel.

The rest of its body was buried in sand, pressed against the rock. It roared when Issa approached and showed its big yellowish teeth.

"Salaam," Issa said quietly. "Peace, Camel. I mean you no harm."

The animal studied the old man suspiciously. Issa dismounted, keeping his distance. He was puzzled. Clearly the camel was kneeling. It should have been strong enough to get to its feet, to lift itself free of the sand and dust, but it had chosen not to. Why?

Then a cry, a tiny cry, leaked into the hot air. The camel turned its head and flared its nostrils. Issa now saw that behind the animal there was a split in the wall of stone, like a very narrow cave. He moved forward, slowly and cautiously, murmuring soft words.

"Easy, Camel, sir, easy. Here, smell my hand. I would prefer it if you did not bite it. Good. Thank you."

Now Issa was close enough to see that the camel's bridle was embroidered in the same black, green and red pattern as the ribbon he had found at sunrise. Except that woven into the bridle were letters. A word.

"Jin-Jin? Is that your name? Jin-Jin?"

The camel's ears swivelled forward. Yes.

"Jin-Jin. Well, Jin-Jin, you must trust me. Please stand up, my friend. Up."

Another thin cry came from within the rock. A human cry.

The camel hesitated, then began to move. Heaving himself free of the sand, unfolding his long legs. Standing. Yet he did not seem to want to leave the wall of rock. Issa took hold of his bridle and made encouraging noises.

"Chuh-chuh-cher. Come, Jin-Jin. Chuh-chuh."

And at last Jin-Jin trusted Issa enough to move. He stepped out into the hot gaze of the sun.

"Good," Issa said, patting the camel's shoulder. "Now let us see what you were so anxious to protect from the storm."

Issa opened the woven basket and his heart stumbled. A child's eyes were looking up at his.

Once, many years earlier, a trader had shown Issa a black pearl. It had a gleam deep inside it. This child, this baby, had huge black pearls for eyes. Her body was wrapped in finest, softest cotton. Something made of gold hung from a cord around her neck, something the shape of half of a star. There were letters hammered into the gold, but Issa could not make sense of them.

The child scrunched her eyes shut and wailed.

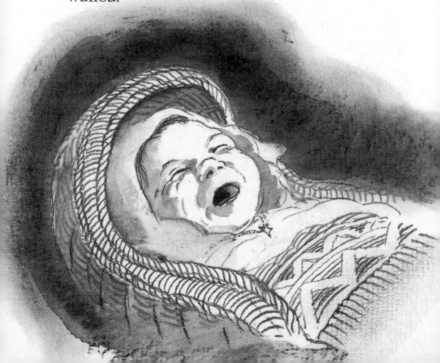

Issa stepped back and looked up at the sky. "Why," he asked it, "did you send such a gift to an old man?"

Issa named the child Mariama and raised her. The townspeople decided that she was his grandchild and he did not deny it. He took her everywhere with him. Before she learned to walk she was familiar with the donkey's jerky trot and Jin-Jin's steady lurch. The travellers and traders who paid Issa to guide them were puzzled that he had a girl child with him. Sometimes they teased him.

And Issa would say, "Mariama is a child of the desert. She comes with us to pay her respects to her family. To her uncles, the rocks and hills. To her aunts, the stars. To her four cousins, the winds. How could I leave her at home, when this is her home?"

Perhaps Issa believed this. Or half believed it. The truth was, though, that love had made them inseparable.

As the years went by, Mariama learned everything that Issa knew: the maps made by the stars, the shimmering paths through the hills, the weather foretold by dawns and sunsets, the messages on the wind, the stories told by stones.

She learned that for a guide everything had a meaning. The shape of a thorn tree, the way sand swirled from the crest of a dune, the length and colour of a shadow, the call of a bird, the height of a cloud.

One evening, Issa was reading aloud from the Quran. He paused in his reading and said, "Please light the lamps, Mariama."

She looked up, puzzled. "The lamps are already lit, Grandfather."

He lifted his head. "Ah, yes," he said. "So they are."

A few mornings later, she watched his hand searching for the bowl of coffee she'd put in front of him. She watched him fumbling to open the gate to the goat pen.

And she understood. Her blood turned as cold as the water from the well.

She waited for him to tell her, and at last he did.

"I am going blind, my child," he said simply. "My old eyes are dying faster than the rest of me."

All Mariama could say was, "Yes, Grandfather. I know."

Darkness descended quickly on Issa. Within a few weeks he was using a stick to feel his way between the house and the stable.

25

One morning, Mariama found him standing by the goat pen fence with his face lifted towards the rising sun.

He said, "Is it beautiful, child?"

"Yes, Baba."

Issa nodded. "Yes. I have a thousand memories of it, thanks be to God, which is enough. But I have been thinking – who will pay a guide who is blind? How will we live?"

Mariama had no answer, so she put her arm around her grandfather's waist. He put his hand on her small shoulder.

After a silence he said, "I found a baby in the desert. It was a sort of miracle. But my first thought was that it was unfair for an old man to be burdened with a child; that trouble had been sent into my life. I was wrong, of course. God has plans that we only understand afterwards, in darkness. You were a gift. I thought the gift was love, but it was even more than that."

"Yes, Baba," Mariama said. "I was sent to be your eyes."

So now Mariama had another skill to learn: how to use words to show Issa the things that his eyes could not see.

"We are below the rock shaped like a lizard," she would say. Or, "The cloud is like the skin of a grey fish." Or, "Now we are passing the line of thorn trees that look like old women lifting their shawls over their heads."

"Yes," Issa might say. "Good, Mariama. That is what they are like. I always thought so."

And in this way, with his long memory and Mariama as his eyes, Issa was still the greatest of all guides. When travellers asked for help, the townspeople said, "You need Issa and his granddaughter. Their house is that way. Look for the crooked gate."

* * *

Then, late one afternoon, three strangers came to the house. One was taller than a door and fierce-looking, with a scar on his face that began beside his left eye and disappeared into his beard. Two other men stood behind him. One was old with a nose like a hawk's beak. The other was young. His dark eyes were restless, as if keen to remember everything they saw. When Mariama asked them to come inside, Scarface and Hawknose stood aside to allow the young man to enter first.

Ah, Mariama thought. So he is the important one.

While she boiled water for tea she studied him, secretly. And if Issa had been able to see, he might have recognized the pattern in the embroidery that trimmed his robes.

Issa and the visitors made a little polite conversation while evening shadows filled

the room. Then Scarface cleared his throat
and got down to business.

"We are heading for Ahara," he said.

Issa nodded. "A tiresome journey, but not
a difficult one. The salt caravans go there all
the time. Team up with one of them. You will
not get lost."

"We do not have time for that," Scarface
said. "The caravans go round the Bitter
Mountains. We want to go through them,
which will save us at least six days' travelling.
We are in a hurry. And we are told that only
you know the way."

"Perhaps," Issa said. "But it is harsh and
dangerous, and there is no water in the
mountains. Besides, I am an old man, as you
see. I do not think I have the strength for
such a journey." He sighed and shook his
head. "Forgive me, but I cannot help you."

Mariama saw Scarface turn to look at the
young man, who made a little gesture with

his head. A gesture that gave permission.

Scarface reached inside his robe and produced a small bag that he dropped into Issa's lap.

"Perhaps this will change your mind," he said.

Mariama watched her grandfather's old but clever fingers untie the little bag and feel what was inside.

Pearls. Issa's fingers counted them. There were a great many. He felt their perfect shape and glossiness. They were like an angel's tears fallen to earth. Priceless.

Recently, when he should have been sleeping, Issa had been worrying about Mariama. What would become of her when he died? How would she live? Who would marry an orphaned girl with no money? Now these questions came into his head once more. And it seemed to him that the heavy little bag in his hand contained the answers. He sighed again.

"Wealth does not always bring happiness," he said finally. "But poverty always brings sorrow. Your offer is too generous to refuse, kind sirs. I will guide you through the Bitter Mountains."

"Thank you," Scarface said. "Excellent."

The visitors finished their tea and got to their feet.

Scarface said, "So, we will meet tomorrow, God willing."

"Yes," Issa said. "At sunrise, God willing. Mariama, fetch me my stick."

She brought it and put it into his hand and helped him to stand. He used the stick to find his way to the door.

An awful silence filled the room.

Hawknose ended it. "Old man, can you not see? Are you blind?"

"Yes," Issa said, surprised. "Did you not know? Were you not told?"

Another silence.

Hawknose narrowed his eyes. "A blind guide? Is this some sort of joke? Some sort of trick?"

Mariama felt hot blood rise to her face. She stepped forward and spoke.

"Sirs, no one has deceived you. My
grandfather knows this land like no other.
As if it were his own hand. I am his eyes.
You can trust us. Ask anyone."

"Pah!" Scarface said, scowling, and tore
the bag of pearls from Issa's hand.
"Let us go, master.
These people
think we are
fools."

The young man said nothing. He looked
into Mariama's eyes for the first time. There

34

was a question in his face but he did not ask it. Then he turned away and led his companions out of the house.

Early the following morning, Mariama went to fetch water from the well.

When she returned Issa said, as usual, "What news, child?"

The village well was the place for gossip. When she went for water, she was her grandfather's ears, too.

Mariama filled the kettle. "They have left," she said. "The young man and the other two. Soon after dawn. Heading for the Bitter Mountains."

"What? Without a guide?"

"Yes. The young man has a magic stone shaped like a finger. When he hangs it from a string it always points to the north. He says he would rather follow his magic stone than a guide who cannot see."

Issa grunted and stroked his chin.

"Birds have the same magic stone in their heads," he said eventually. "That is how they find their way. But birds can fly over mountains and over seas. Men cannot."

The old man took his stick and tapped his way out into the yard. Mariama followed him. He lifted his face to the sky. He licked his finger and held it up to measure the wind.

Mariama waited.

"Saddle Jin-Jin," Issa said at last. "And prepare us for a journey. Make haste, child."

The sun had already begun its climb down the sky when Mariama brought Jin-Jin to a halt. Her sharp eyes studied the sandy, stony ground.

"They left the caravan route here, Baba. They turned north, towards the mountains."

Issa tutted his tongue against his teeth. "Can you read their tracks?"

"Yes, I think so."

"Good. We'll follow."

Late in the afternoon, they stopped again. The twisting trail had taken them, slowly, higher and higher. Now the ground beneath the camel's feet was hard rock. Mariama could no longer see the travellers' tracks.

"I have lost them, Baba," she confessed.

"Hmm. Perhaps," Issa said. "Tell me where we are. Tell me what you see."

A valley lay ahead of them. Its walls were of great brown rock piled up like books that might belong to a giant. In their shadows, big-bellied baobab trees lifted their thick branches and fingery leaves into the air like a row of fat old ladies dancing. In the distance beyond the valley, huge towers of rock rose into the air, carved into fantastic shapes by the desert winds. In the late sun they looked as though they had been cut from purple paper and glued to the sky.

Mariama described all this to her grandfather.

He nodded approvingly, then asked, "How much of the day is left?"

The western sky was turning the colour of a sea-coral bracelet.

"Only an hour," Mariama said.

The old man grunted. "So," he said. "Look down into the valley. Can you see a big rock the shape of a boat, balanced on another rock? Looking as if it should fall?"

"Yes, Grandfather. I see it."

"Good. We will camp there for the night."

In the morning, her grandfather shook Mariama awake. The stars were fading into the dawn. She blew life back into the fire and she and Issa sat close to it wrapped in their blankets.

After a while Issa said, "Is it light enough to see yet?"

"Yes, Grandfather, just."

He pointed with his stick. "Can you see a little path over there, going up? Yes? Follow it to the top of the cliff, then come back and tell me what you saw. And be careful, child."

Mariama climbed the steep path. It was just a crack in the rock. In places it was only a little wider than her body. When at last she reached the top, she stood staring, hardly able to breathe.

The mountains stretched before her to the very edge of distance. Some had peaks that were flat-topped and grooved like huge and ancient teeth. Others were bent and twisted like goats' horns, while others were slender and pointed like minarets. And they were all a deep, dark blue, like the scarves of the camel traders who came from the north. But then, as Mariama watched, the light of the rising sun touched the tips of the mountains and painted them a glowing, burning gold.

She cried out aloud, because she had
never seen anything so beautiful, so magical.
And as the sun climbed higher, the golden
light slid down the teeth, the horns, the
minarets. The blue drained away, and now
she saw that dark valleys curled among the
mountains like the roots of a tree. And from
one of these valleys, not far away, arose
a little twist of smoke.

She turned and hurried down the cliff path.

Issa was standing waiting for her. "What did you see?"

"I cannot describe it, Baba. I do not have the words."

Her grandfather smiled. "No. I have stood where you stood, trying to think in words. But tell me, did you see smoke?"

"Yes."

"In which direction? How far away?"

Mariama told him.

"Yes," Issa said, "that would be the strangers' fire. These valleys are a maze, and already they are lost. Now, let us make coffee."

"But, Grandfather, should we not set off after the travellers, if they are lost?"

"No. That valley is a dead end. They will have to return the way they went. We have time for breakfast. Then we will go to meet them."

Issa was wrong. Perhaps, if his eyes had been good, he would have seen that the sun had a cloudy grey belly when it rose above the mountains.

They had been riding for an hour when he said, "Hss, Jin-Jin. Stop."

Mariama looked at him. "What is it, Baba?"

Issa did not answer. The silence that surrounded them was as thick as a fleece. No birds called from the thorn trees. No insects hissed or chirruped from the rocks.

"Grandfather?"

"The wind is wrong," Issa said, as if talking to himself. "What colour is the sky?"

Looking up, Mariama saw that it was as white as paper. A flock of desert sparrows flew across it, panicking.

Jin-Jin tossed his head and groaned. Suddenly Mariama was afraid.

"On," Issa said. "Hurry."

They climbed out of one valley and rode

down into the next. In the distance, three shapes wobbled in the heat haze.

"There!" Mariama cried. "I can see them, Baba! They are coming back this way, just as you said they would."

Mariama urged Jin-Jin onwards to meet the travellers, but he resisted. He groaned deep in his throat and tried to turn back.

And then Mariama saw why.

The lower edge of the sky had changed again; now it was yellowy-purple, the colour of an old bruise. A hot and sudden gust of wind, full of grit, hit Mariama in the face.

The riders had felt it too. They looked over their shoulders then whipped their camels into a gallop. A boiling brown cloud loomed over the valley.

"A sandstorm, Grandfather!" Mariama cried. "A sandstorm, coming at us!"

"I feared so," Issa said grimly. "Now listen to me, child. Look over to our right. Can you see a split in the cliff, like a tall shadow?"

"I can see many, Grandfather."

"Look again. Can you see one that is darker than the others? One bent like a dog's leg?" His voice was calm and steady.

The riders were close now, but the storm was swarming into the valley behind them like a pack of hungry wolves.

Mariama swallowed her fear and studied
the face of the cliff.

"Yes," she said. "I see it."

"Good," her grandfather said. "That is our
place of safety. Take us there, Mariama. And
make this stubborn camel run like the wind!"

"This way!" Mariama yelled, pointing.
"Follow us!"

The three travellers hesitated, their eyes wide with fear; but when Mariama turned Jin-Jin and charged towards the cliff, they followed. Sand lifted from the ground in stinging whirlwinds. The sky darkened and moaned.

When they reached the cliff, Mariama's heart sank. The gap in the rock seemed hardly big enough to shelter one camel, let alone four. She turned to Issa, the flying sand biting her face.

"We have come to the wrong place, Baba! There is nothing here!"

Issa slid from Jin-Jin's back to the ground.

"Trust me, child," he said, and felt for the camel's reins. "And you, Jin-Jin, sir, must trust me too."

The split in the rock was narrow, but deeper than Mariama had thought. Issa led them into it, feeling his way with his hand. The harsh stone scraped Jin-Jin's flanks. He groaned and lowered his head but went on. Mariama was afraid; she felt as though the huge cliff were closing in on her, crushing her. Then, suddenly, they were in a great space. A cave! Thin beams of light from the opening lit up its sandy floor, but its walls and roof were lost in darkness.

One by one the three travellers followed them in, soothing their nervous camels as they entered the cool darkness. Scarface was the last. He looked about him and began to say something but his words were lost in a great wave of sound. The desert storm roared past the cave and filled it with deafening noise. The last beams of sunlight went out like snuffed candles.

A long hour passed. Then at last the storm, with a final whip of its tail, vanished into the distance. Silently, daylight spread its fingers into the cave.

The young man was the first to speak.
"Thanks be to God."

"Indeed," Issa said. "Now Mariama will
lead us home. Then, when you and your
animals are rested, you can set off again for
Ahara. And this time, I think, you will take
the safe route around the mountains, yes?"

Two mornings later, the young traveller
came again to Issa's house. This time he was
alone. When Mariama let him in, he bowed
to her and smiled. Blushing, she put the
kettle on the stove to make coffee, then sat
in her corner of the room.

The young man had come, he said,
to show his gratitude and to beg Issa's
forgiveness. He apologized for his men
mocking Issa's blindness, for their insults.
He praised Issa's knowledge of the desert.
He congratulated Issa on the bravery
and intelligence of his granddaughter,

which made Mariama blush again.

"My comrades and I are about to leave," he said. "I came to say farewell and to give you this." He lifted Issa's hand and put the pouch of pearls into it. The old man felt it with his fingers, then handed it back.

"I cannot accept this," he said. "I did not guide you to Ahara."

"No. You did much more than that. You saved our lives."

"Yes, praise God," Issa said. "But not for payment."

The young man frowned, uncertain what to do. Then he went to Mariama and placed the pouch on the floor close to her. He held his finger to his lips, bidding her to say nothing. Then he froze, staring down at her.

"Where did you get that?" he demanded. "The gold pendant you wear around your neck."

His voice was suddenly stern, and
Mariama was alarmed. Her hand flew
to the pendant as if to protect it.

"Tell me," the young man insisted.
"I have always had it, sir. I was wearing
it when ... when Grandfather found me."

"Found you? What do you mean, *found you*?"

Mariama bit her lip. There were things that only she and Baba knew. Was she now to share them with this stranger?

Issa came to her rescue. He said quietly, "I think the pendant has a special meaning for you. Am I right, sir?"

"Yes," the traveller said. His eyes remained fixed on Mariama.

Issa nodded. "Please sit," he said, "and I will tell you a story. Or perhaps half a story. It is possible that you know the other half."

So the young man sat beside Mariama while the old man told him how, after a great storm, he had found a bad-tempered camel protecting a baby. That he had brought the child to his house and raised her. He had always known that the gold pendant marked her out as someone special. That she was a gift that might one day be taken from him.

Then he said, "Are you the one who has come to take her from me?"

Mariama sat folded in a kind of terror. The familiar room suddenly felt strange to her.

Instead of answering Issa's question, the young traveller said, "My name is Abbas. My father is the king of Sana, which borders the Eastern Sea. When I was a boy, ten thousand warriors attacked my father's kingdom. Thinking that he would lose this war, my father sent me north to my uncle's house, where I would be safe. He sent my sister, who was then just a baby, to our other uncle, who lived at the edge of the Great Desert.

"After many battles, my father and his armies beat the attackers off and saved the kingdom. He sent word for his children to be returned. I was brought home but my sister could not be found. She had never reached our uncle's house. She and the warriors protecting her had vanished somewhere on their journey. My father could not bring himself to believe that she was dead. We have been looking for her ever since."

Issa had listened intently to Abbas's words. He nodded his head slowly, then spoke.

"And how will you know her, if you find her?"

Abbas reached inside his robe and pulled free a gold pendant that hung from his neck by a leather cord. He lifted the cord over his head and held the pendant in his left hand.

"She will be wearing the other half of this." He reached his right hand out to Mariama. "Please," he said gently.

She removed her own pendant and gave it to him. Abbas put the two together. Now they formed a perfect eight-pointed star,

and the hammered letters formed the words
Children of Sana, Children of God.

Mariama stared, wide-eyed.

Understanding filled her, like a sunrise.

Abbas said, "Hello, my sister. It has been
a long time. Today we have mended our
father's heart." And he wrapped his arms
around her and held her close.

Tearful rejoicing filled the small room.

"We will leave tomorrow," Abbas said with laughter in his voice. "I cannot wait to see our father's face. There will be a great feast!"

Mariama's smile clouded over. "Leave? But I can't. Grandfather needs me. I cannot leave him here alone."

"Nonsense," Issa said gruffly. "I shall manage perfectly well."

"No, Baba. I won't go."

Abbas put his hands on Mariama's shoulders. "Of course you cannot leave your grandfather."

He went to the old man and kneeled. "Sir," he said. "You must come with us. Stay with us as our honoured guest for as long as you wish. No, please do not argue. My father's palace is a beautiful place, with the great green river on one side and the silver sea on the other. Its courtyards are cool, shaded by trees that blossom all the year round, their flowers white and yellow and blue. There are fountains that throw fans of glittering water into the air. All this will be yours to enjoy."

Issa smiled. "It does indeed sound beautiful," he said, "but you seem to forget. I will not be able to see it."

"Yes, you will, Baba," Mariama said. "You will see it through my eyes."

And that is exactly what happened.

Night Sky Dragons

The boy clomped across the yard in his heavy winter boots, scattering the fluffed-up and sulky chickens. He stomped up the steps to the walkway that ran inside the high walls of the han. He climbed the ladder that rose to the ramparts above the huge wood and iron gates and squinted out at the world. His face was small under his knitted cap and above the collar of his goatskin coat. It looked like a fingertip poking through a hole in a glove.

The watchmen smiled when they greeted him.

"Ho, Yazul! You're up early. You're expecting someone?"

The low red sun spilled light into the valley and painted purple shadows on the endless, snow-smothered mountains that surrounded it.

"No," Yazul said. "I thought perhaps spring might have come."

The taller watchman shook his head. "No, not yet, Yazul. It's late this year. But soon. I can almost smell it."

* * *

The han stood in its valley halfway between
the two ends of the world. In one direction,
far, far beyond the sunrise, were the lands
of the Great Emperor. That was where all the
wonderful things came from. In the other
direction, far, far beyond the sunset, was the
Great City. That was where all the wonderful
things were put on ships that sailed beyond
the limits of Yazul's imagination.

Within the han's high walls travellers
and merchant caravans found shelter.
A place to rest and trade. A place of safety
too. Between the ends of the world there
were many dangers.

* * *

Yazul sniffed the sharp air.

When spring came, it would come with magical swiftness. It would bring streams of clear, cold water, snow melt from the hills. It would bring the warm winds perfect for kite-flying.

Soon. But not yet.

Yazul sighed, and shivered. He would go and see if Grandpa was awake.

In his grandfather's workshop the fire was already crackling inside the brick stove. Later it would melt a pot of thick yellow glue; but for now it warmed the tea kettle.

"Pour yourself a bowl," his grandfather said. "The cold has turned your nose white."

He smiled, and when he smiled the blue bird tattooed on his cheek shrugged its wings. This was one of the many reasons Yazul loved him.

Through the tea steam rising from his
bowl, Yazul looked around the workshop.
Long stems of bamboo. Shelves of clay pots
containing paint and ink and dye. Rolls
of silk on wooden rods. Fat balls of twine.
Sheets of precious paper. The tools and
brushes laid out in the proper order. This
room was Yazul's favourite place, the safest
place in his small world. Here, after his
mother died, his grandfather had taught
him, patiently, the art of building kites and
the skill of flying them. Gradually, Yazul
had discovered that the kites could lift his
sadness into the sky, where the
wind would carry it away,
little by little.

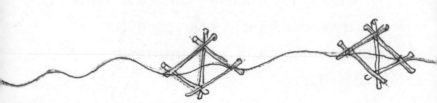

Hanging from the workshop ceiling was
the hawk kite Yazul and his grandfather had
worked on yesterday. They had spent the
whole day steaming and shaping the bamboo
into a pair of broad wings and a tail like a fan.

Grandpa finished his tea and went to the
rolls of silks. He rubbed his hands. "Now
then. What colour is our hawk, Yazul? Black?
Orange?"

"Blue," Yazul said. "Blue like
the sky in spring."

* * *

When the kite was finished, Yazul took it to show his father. His father was the lord of the han. Loneliness had made him stern, so although Yazul loved him, he also feared him a little.

Yazul displayed the kite proudly.

"A fine kite," his father said.

Yazul smiled.

"Another fine kite," his father added. His voice was cold. Yazul's smile froze on his face. His father went to the window and stared out at the empty valley.

"One day I will die, Yazul. Then this han will be yours to protect. And all the people in it.

You will need to be a man, and strong."

Yazul did not know what to say, so he said nothing.

His father turned to face him.

"Business, Yazul. Business. Money. That is the real world. That is food in your belly. That is warm clothes on your back. Travel and trade are what matter."

"Yes, Father."

A silence fell between them.

It ended when his father said, "I respect your grandfather, Yazul. I kneeled before him when I asked his permission to marry your mother. But now he is an old man, and old men have time on their hands. Time to daydream. Or to fly kites, which is another kind of dreaming. But you are young, my son. Too young to live in dreams. There is nothing in the sky. Put your feet on the earth. Do you understand what I am telling you?"

"Yes, Father. I understand."

Yazul returned to the workshop with a troubled heart. His father's love was a sad and heavy thing. Kites rode the air and made him happy. It seemed he could not have both. But he was too small for such enormous choices.

His grandfather asked, "Did your father like the kite?"

"Yes. He said it was a fine kite."

But Yazul did not look at his grandfather when he said this.

There was mischief in Yazul, a love of tricks. For example, he had learned that if you cut sections of bamboo in a certain way and put them into the fire of the stove, they would explode. The air inside the hollow stems would swell in the heat and burst with a wonderful bang.

When he did this his grandfather would put a hand on his chest and cry, "Dragon!

Save us, gods! Save us from the fire dragon!"
Then he would slump to the floor and
pretend to be dead.

"It was me, Grandpa," Yazul would say,
smiling. "Just me, not a dragon."

Then his grandfather would open one eye
and the blue bird would shrug its wings.

But one day, not long before spring came to
the valley, this trick went terribly wrong. Yazul
was alone in the workshop. He was bored,
so he went to the pile of unwanted bits of
bamboo and found a nice thick one. He put it
into the stove and shut the fire door. When the
explosion came it was his best ever; the glue
pot on top of the stove hopped. But it wasn't
the bang that made Yazul whirl round. It was
the crash and the scream that followed it.

His grandmother stood just outside the
workshop door holding her hands to her
face. Her eyes were shocked wide open.

"It's all right, Grandma," Yazul said. "It wasn't a dragon; it was..."

Then his voice died in his mouth, because he saw what lay at his grandmother's feet.

A dish, a big one. Shattered into jagged pieces.

Fear filled Yazul like a winter sickness.
Because this dish was, or had been, no
ordinary dish. It was the history of his
people. Coiling round its edge and into its
centre were delicate pictures in blue and
brown and white. They told the story of his
ancestors. The story of the old ones who had
been swallowed up by time. Their troubles
and travels, their marriages and great
moments, had been painted onto the dish.
Many hands whose bones were now dust had
worked on it. From his earliest childhood,
Yazul had sat with his grandmother while
her old fingers traced the tales and recited
the names. His eyes had grown wide when
she pointed to the dragons that appeared
in the sky when the gods were angry.

The dish was older than memory.
It was his grandmother's most valued
possession. And now Yazul's foolishness
had destroyed it.

His grandmother looked at him. Her eyes were full of tears now, and her voice was broken.

"Yazul, Yazul. What have you done?"

He could not speak. His grandfather appeared, his face full of anxiety. When he saw the shards on the ground his face turned to stone. He squatted and studied them.

Yazul made his voice work. "Can you mend it, Grandpa?"

"No," the old man said. "No, I do not think so."

His grandmother turned away from Yazul and spoke to the sky. "It is a sign. Our family has come to its end."

"Nonsense, superstitious nonsense," the old man said. "It is a broken dish and nothing more."

But he did not look at his grandson when he said this.

Yazul's father's rage was as cold and fierce as a storm in the mountains.

"It is idleness that has made you so foolish," he said. "Come with me."

He led Yazul to the kitchen and summoned the cook.

"This boy is your new drudge," he said. "Work him hard."

The kitchen servants did not dare mistreat or abuse Yazul. But they made sure he was given the filthiest tasks, and grinned behind their hands while he laboured at them.

When spring came, Yazul did not smell it.
Nor did he launch a kite into the rising wind.
He was carrying buckets of slop to the pigs.
When the meltwater tumbled into the valley,
he did not hear it. He was raking ashes
from the cook stoves, coughing. When the
first caravans of the season arrived, he did
not go with his father to greet them. While
the courtyard filled with the neighing and
bellowing of the pack animals, while their
precious cargoes were unloaded into the

han's strongrooms, Yazul was on his knees, scrubbing the kitchen's cold stone floor.

Weeks of slavery dragged by. Then, on an afternoon when the sun was a white disc hanging in the sky, a shout came from the ramparts of the han.

"Caravan! A caravan coming from the east!"

Yazul's father hurried up the steps and stared into the distance, shading his eyes with his hand. The watchman pointed.

"There, my lord. Do you see them? They're raising a lot of dust. They're moving fast."

"Yes. I wonder why they are riding so hard."

A cry from further along the wall: "Other riders, my lord! Away to the left!"

And yes, there was a second long cloud of dust moving along the higher ground, pursuing the hurrying caravan.

"Bandits, my lord?"

"Perhaps," Yazul's father said quietly. He turned and yelled orders down to the courtyard. "Make ready at the gates! Archers, to your positions!"

The quiet afternoon was shattered by a clamour of shouts and frantic activity.

The caravan reached the safety of the han only moments ahead of its pursuers. The great gates slammed shut behind it, and the three massive iron bars that fastened them

were heaved into place. The courtyard was
a chaos of men and animals. The travellers
– merchants, their servants and guards –
had faces masked by dust and streaked with
sweat. Their long-haired and heavily laden
camels drooled ropes of foam from their
muzzles. They were panicky, and did not
know what to do with their huge feet. Their
riders struggled to control them. From the
kitchen doorway Yazul and the servants
gazed at all this with huge eyes.

Up on the ramparts the lord of the han
called out, "Do not shoot! Save your arrows!"

His archers relaxed their bowstrings. The
bandits, fifty or sixty of them, had reined in
their horses just beyond the range of arrow
shot. Fierce men with beards greased into
rat-tails, swords sheathed on their backs,
bows hanging from their saddles, quivers
of arrows close to their knees. They sat
silently on their horses, watching, while the

dust settled around them. Then they slowly circled the han, studying it. Looking for its weaknesses.

Yazul's father walked along the walls, watching them watching him. He touched the backs of his men, steadying them.

When night fell, the bandits lit fires and rode in front of them, calling out taunts to the han. Offering its people choices of ways they might die.

Yazul's father called a meeting of the elders.

"They will not attack," he said. "They will lose men if they do. They will not shoot fire arrows to burn us out, because the fire would destroy the things they want to steal. They will wait. They will hunt in the hills and drink from the river, knowing that we cannot. With so many new people in the han, we will soon run out of food and water. Their plan is to starve us into surrender."

"Yes," Yazul's grandfather said. "And what is worse is that other caravans will come here expecting shelter. Instead, they will be attacked. And when this becomes known, caravans from west and east will avoid us. We will have no way to live."

"True. So what should we do?"

No one could answer this question.

Many days passed, each one seeming longer than the last. The bandits waited, patient as wolves. Inside the han, camels and horses groaned their thirst. Hunger turned the people sullen and silent. In the nights they were tormented by the smell of meat cooking over the bandits' fires.

One morning, Yazul heard his father talking to the cook.

"We can last four more days, my lord," the cook said. "Perhaps five. There is very little food left."

"And water?"

"Almost gone, my lord. We have stopped watering the animals."

That night, after another hopeless meeting of the elders, Yazul tugged his grandfather's sleeve in the darkness of the courtyard.

"Grandpa, I want to talk with you. I have an idea."

Yazul whispered into the old man's ear, then waited. In the dark he could not see his grandfather's face. He could not see if the blue bird moved its wings.

"Hmm," his grandfather said at last. "It might work. Yes, it might just work. I'll go and speak with your father."

85

Yazul's father scoffed. "More foolishness, Father-in-law," he said. "More boys' games."

"Perhaps. But older and wiser heads have not come up with anything better."

The lord of the han grunted and stared moodily into the fire.

"Very well," he said. "Now that there is little for him to do in the kitchen, it will at least keep the boy from mischief."

For three days and two nights Yazul, his grandfather and their helpers toiled in the workshop. The eight kites they built were bigger and stronger than any they had made before: taller than a man and wider than outspread arms.

And black as a starless night. Black-dyed silk,
black-painted bamboo frames, flying lines
blackened with ink. On each one the old
man painted huge red dragon eyes and red
dragon mouths with ferocious teeth.

"Is this right, Yazul? Is this how you
imagined them? Are they scary enough?"

"Yes, Grandpa."

"Good," the old man said. "They scare me."
The blue bird on his cheek lifted its wings.

87

Each kite had a long, long tail of black twine soaked in oil. Threaded onto these tails were slender sections of bamboo the length of Yazul's hand.

"Will it work, Grandpa? Will they burn?"

"Hmm," his grandfather murmured, twiddling his beard. "I'm not sure."

Yazul waited anxiously while a long minute passed. Then the old man went over to a cabinet in the corner and rummaged.

"It's here somewhere," he muttered. "Is that it? No... Ah!"

He came back to the workbench and set down a fat pot with a narrow neck and a tight stopper. Then he picked up a sharp spike with a wooden handle and began to bore a small hole into the first piece of bamboo on the tail of a kite.

"What are you doing, Grandpa?"

"This is my little addition to your plan,

Yazul. Pass me that scrap of paper. Yes, that one. Good. Now, watch."

The old man shaped the paper into a funnel and teased the thin end into the hole he had bored. Next, with a struggle, he pulled the stopper from the fat pot.

"A man from the east traded me this," he said. "I did not like him much. He told me that it would change the world, but I never found a use for it until now."

From the pot he tipped a pinch of brown powder into the funnel, tapping the paper with his finger.

"Pah," he murmured. "It stinks."

When the last grains of powder had trickled into the bamboo,

Yazul's grandfather removed the funnel and sealed the hole with a blob of warm wax.

"There," he said. "Do you think you can do that?"

"Yes, I think so. But why, Grandpa? What is that stuff?"

His grandfather raised one eyebrow. "Aren't you Yazul? Aren't you the boy who loves tricks and surprises?"

When the last of the powder had been tipped into the last piece of bamboo on the last of the kite tails, Yazul's grandfather sat down wearily.

"I want you all to leave me now," he said. "I need to speak to the sky gods. I need to beg them for a dark night and a strong and well-shaped wind."

It seemed that the gods had listened, and been generous. That night, when the great black kites were carried silently up onto the walls of the han, not a single star peeped over the sky's dark blanket. The wind ran out of the west, strong and eager.

The bandits' campfires had burned low, just yellow smudges in the darkness. The men on the walls waited until the only sound in the valley was an occasional snicker or snuffle from the horses. Yazul looked over to where his father stood, at the far end of the ramparts, but it was too dark to read the expression on his face.

At last Yazul's grandfather murmured, "It is time."

It was not an easy task, launching the kites. As soon as they were lifted upright they strained to fly. It took two men to hold each one, and a third, bracing himself, to hold the handles of the flying lines. The black silk hissed and rippled.

"Now," Grandpa called hoarsely. "Release them!"

One kite failed to climb onto the wind. It tumbled, and dangled against the gates like a huge and wounded bat. The other seven soared like black ghosts into the

black sky. As they rose, their tails played
out, the bamboo clattering softly against
the stone parapet.

"Catch those tails," Yazul's grandfather
hissed urgently. "Don't let them go!"

Yazul stared out towards the bandits' camp. Nothing stirred. No cries of alarm disturbed the night.

His grandfather scuttled along the wall, whispering questions and instructions.

"Steady. Good, like that. Keep your hands level. Can you feel what the kite is telling you? Is all the string reeled out?"

"Yes."

"Yes."

"By the gods, old man, it pulls like a bull."

"Good, good. Yazul – the burners."

Yazul picked up the two iron pots of glowing charcoal. He and his grandfather took each kite tail and held it in the embers, blowing breath onto them till the string caught fire. One by one, little worms of flame climbed into the sky.

For a short time that felt like a year, nothing happened.

"Let it work," Yazul prayed. "Please let it work."

And then he clamped his hand over his mouth to stifle a cry. Above the bandits' camp, a bright explosion cracked and flowered. Then another. And as the fuses burned from one bamboo firecracker to the next, igniting the gunpowder, another and another. The darkness was split by furious bangs and flashes, and each flash lit up the red eyes and teeth of the dragons hanging in the night.

Yells and howls of fear erupted from the bandits' camp.

"Dragons!"

"Sky dragons!"

"The gods have turned against us!"

Worse still was the terror of their horses. They pranced in panic, tore their tethers from the ground and raced, whinnying and whirling, in all directions.

When the echo of the blast of the last night sky dragon faded, the valley filled

with a silence so deep that Yazul could
almost touch it.

In the first light of morning, Yazul's father
led twelve armed men through the gates
of the han and out into the valley. It was
empty. Cautiously, they walked their horses
through the yellow and white and pink
flowers to where the bandits had camped.
They found fire beds of dead grey ash,
abandoned bedrolls, discarded weapons,

and seven black silk kites lying flat on
the ground.

Yazul's father returned to the han and
dismounted in the courtyard, where Yazul
and his grandfather stood waiting. He
looked at his son as if he had never seen the
boy before. Then he nodded, and his face
opened into a smile. It was the first time
Yazul had seen his father smile for a very
long time. It was like the longed-for arrival
of spring after a hard winter.

His father stooped and lifted Yazul onto his shoulders. Instantly the han was a hubbub of cheers and shouts. Yazul's name echoed and re-echoed from the walls, and he was so full of happiness that he almost could not breathe. But even as he rode on his father's shoulders around the courtyard, even as hands rose to shake his hand and slap his back, there was a part of Yazul's mind that was somewhere else. It was fixed on the difficult task ahead of him.

It took almost a month of painstaking care, and when it was finished he was not satisfied, even though he knew that it was the best he could do. He carried the dish to his grandmother and, kneeling, laid it in her lap.

"I am sorry," he said. "It is not perfect. You see, here and here?"

The old woman ran her thin fingers over its surface. Her lips moved silently.

Yazul waited.

"No," she said, "it is not perfect. It is better than perfect. Look here. Look closely."

His grandmother's finger traced a pattern of cracks in the dish that Yazul's care had failed to conceal.

"You see? It is a kite. You did not mean to make yourself part of this story, but you did. You will live in memory for ever, as the boy who saved us with his night sky dragons."

Cloud Tea Monkeys

One by one, the familiar sounds of morning drew Tashi from her sleep. Her mother breathing life into the fire; the hiss and crackle of the twigs as the flames caught; the whispering of the soot-blackened kettle as the water came to the boil.

Tashi took her bowl of sweet tea outside and stood beside the rough road in the blue morning. The sun had not yet found a way through the mountains, but it was coming; a light the colour of lemons was soaking into the sky and painting out the stars.

The air was very cold. Tashi shivered and pulled her shawl more tightly around her. As the stars went out, small squares of light appeared on the dark hillside above her: lamps were being lit in the village. A cockerel crowed and another answered. Inside the house, her mother coughed, twice.

It was not long before Tashi heard voices and laughter from where the road curved down from the hill. Then the women came, their white headscarves glowing in the half-dark, their clothes bright patches of scarlet, green, indigo. Each woman carried a great wicker basket, bigger than Tashi. They called her name, their voices wobbly in the cold air. Her mother came out of the house, her back bent under the burden of her tea basket.

The walk to the tea plantation was long, but for Tashi this was a happy part of the day. The women gossiped and made jokes about their husbands. The sun was kind too,

laying warm patches in the road that were good to walk into out of the cold shadows. Later the sun would turn cruel, burning down from a hazy sky.

When Tashi and her mother and the women arrived at the tea plantation, the Overseer came out of his hut, yawning and scratching his belly. He was a bad-tempered man with a beaky nose and eyes like sharp little stones.

The women stood silently while he told them what they already knew, what they had always known: to pick only the young leaves and the buds from the tops of each bush. Then they found their places and began, plucking the tender leaves and buds and tossing them over their shoulders into their great wicker baskets.

The rows of glossy green tea bushes curved into the distance like waves. Tashi had never seen the end of the plantation. Perhaps it had no end. Perhaps it went right around the world.

Within an hour the sun had sucked the mist up out of the valleys and hung it like a great grey curtain over the peaks of the mountains. Up there, on those wild mountain tops above the clouds, were things Tashi was afraid of: big cats with jade green eyes and snakes like yellow whips.

The monkeys came down into the plantation late in the morning. Tashi knew they had arrived when she heard the Overseer shouting like a crazy man and beating a tin cooking pot with a stick to drive them away. The women squealed and held their skirts tight to their legs as the monkeys, showing their teeth in grins of fear, fled down the rows. The big male monkey that Tashi called Rajah came first, then after him the younger males, and after them the mothers with their babies hanging beneath them or riding on their backs like jockeys in a horse race. Tashi grabbed her lunch bag and followed them.

Tashi and the monkeys met in their usual place, where the endless rows of tea bushes were broken by a jumble of rocks and a tree spread its shadow on the ground. Here she sat and crossed her legs. The monkeys watched her with their deep, serious eyes.

After a while the youngest ones left their mothers and came over to her. There was fruit in her lunch bag and she shared it. The young monkeys inspected Tashi's fingers one by one. With their own long, delicate fingers they groomed her thick dark hair. The mothers relaxed, trusting her. They snoozed in small groups or flirted with the young males. Rajah stalked around the edge of the tree shadow, watching everything.

The women stopped work when the sun was a blurred red globe hanging just above the tea bushes. There was less talk on the way home. The women's tiredness was like a cloud around them. Tashi's mother had bruised-looking eyes. Her cough was worse. Once or twice she stopped and pressed her hand to her chest.

The next morning, there was no crackle from the fire, no whisper from the kettle, no perfume of sweet tea.

"Tashi! Come here, child."

Tashi crossed the dim room to her mother's bed. Her cough was hard and sharp like a stick breaking. Her mother's face was cold but also wet with sweat.

"I am sick, child. I do not think I can work today."

Tashi ran to the dawn-lit road when she heard the women coming. Two came into the house: her Aunt Sonam, and one other. They felt her mother's forehead and spoke to each other in low voices. Sonam brought water and told Tashi to make sure her mother drank. Then they hurried away to their work.

The next morning was the same. Tashi knew that if her mother could not work, there would be no money. With no money to pay the doctor, her mother would not get well. If her mother did not get well, she could not work and there would be no money. The problem went round and round. It was like a snake with its tail in its mouth and Tashi was frightened by it.

When her mother had fallen asleep again, Tashi dragged the heavy tea basket to the door. She found that if she leaned her body forward she could lift the bottom of the basket off the ground. Bent like this she began the long walk to the plantation.

When she got there, Tashi could see no one; the bushes loomed above her. She could hear the shouts of the Overseer and the calls of the women. She hauled the basket along the rows until she saw Aunt Sonam plucking the buds and dropping the leaves over her shoulder into her basket, again and again, like a clockwork machine.

Before Tashi could reach Sonam, a shadow fell upon her. She looked up. The Overseer stood there, his hands on his hips. Desperately Tashi began to pick leaves, any leaves that she could reach.

The Overseer laughed an ugly laugh full of brown teeth. He called the other women to come and look at this stupid child who thought she could pick tea from bushes that were taller than she was. And then he kicked the basket over, spilling the sad and dusty leaves onto the ground. Tashi looked up into the face of her Aunt Sonam, but there was no help there. Sonam did not dare make an enemy of the Overseer, and she pulled an end of her headscarf over her face and turned away.

Tashi dragged the empty basket down to the shade of the tree that grew out of the rocks, and when she got there she sat and wept with her head in her hands. She wept for her mother and for Aunt Sonam and for herself. She cried for a long time. Then she wiped her wet eyes with the backs of her hands and looked up. The monkeys were sitting in the circle of shade, watching her. They were all watching her – the babies hanging from their mothers, the older ones quiet for once, Rajah himself sitting looking at her with his old head tilted curiously to one side. So she told them everything. She told them everything because there was no one else to tell.

When she had finished, there was stillness
and silence for a few moments. Then Rajah
walked through the tree shadow towards her,
coming closer than he had ever come before.
He stood and was suddenly taller than
Tashi. He put his long fingers on the rim of
the basket and felt along it carefully. Then,
without moving his head, he gave a harsh
cry: *"Chack! Chack-chack-chack!"*

Instantly several of the adult
monkeys leaped across the
clearing, grabbed the basket,
lifted it and then, with
amazing strength
and speed,

carried it up and over the jumbled rocks
towards the slopes of the mountains.
Higher and higher they went, Rajah leading.
In a very short time, they and the basket
had vanished into the clouds far above
the plantation.

Tashi was too dismayed by the theft of her mother's basket to cry out. She stood watching the monkeys go, and then sat, feeling terribly tired. The young ones came to her. She took the three small bananas that were her lunch and shared them. Feeding the young ones calmed her. After a while she fell asleep.

She was awakened by a great outburst of screeching and whooping. The adults were back, and they were excited, bouncing from branch to rock and rock to branch, calling loudly. The young ones fled from Tashi's lap to their mothers; the mothers scolded the males for their madness. Rajah sat in the middle of the shade, ignoring all monkey business. He was watching Tashi. The basket stood beside him. She went to it and looked in.

The basket was almost full of small budding sprigs of tea, and Tashi knew

straight away that it was unusual. The leaves
were the colour of emeralds and spangled
with tiny droplets of water, so that the
basket seemed full of green light and a rich
sweet scent.

The basket was even harder to manage now that it was full. It took Tashi a long time to drag it through the baking heat between the endless rows of bushes. When she came into the clearing around the Overseer's hut, surprise stopped her dead. The tea pickers were standing in a long line behind their baskets, whispering and giggling nervously.

Tashi hauled her basket over to where her aunt stood at the end of the line. Sonam glanced down at the child with big astonished eyes but did not speak.

The Overseer was marching about. He looked like a man whose brains were on fire. "Silence!" he yelled. "Silence! Stand straight! Be quiet!"

But it was not the Overseer's mad behaviour that interested Tashi. In the open space beside the hut was a cart with two wooden wheels. The two enormous oxen that had pulled it to the plantation

stood twitching their tails at bothersome
flies. The driver was a very small man
wearing a white turban, and he seemed
to be asleep.

In the cart was a chair with cushions and
a tall back, like a throne. It had a canopy of
purple silk. And in the chair, in the purple
shadow of the purple silk, sat a man made
of silver light like the moon.

The Overseer spoke. "We are honoured,"
he said. "We are very, very honoured to be
visited today by His Excellency the Royal
Tea Taster himself!" The Overseer turned
and made a creepy crouching gesture
towards the man who looked like the moon.
"As you know, His Excellency the Royal Tea
Taster travels the whole world to find teas
that are good enough to be drunk by Her
Majesty the Empress!"

The tea pickers whispered to one another.
The Overseer went dark in the face.

"Silence! His Excellency the Royal Tea Taster will now examine the tea in each of your baskets. And I am sure, quite sure, that he will find that the tea we grow on our plantation is the finest in the world."

The Royal Tea Taster pulled himself up from his throne and stood in the sunlight. Now Tashi could see him clearly. Gold threads glittered in his blue turban, and his long white coat was so heavily embroidered with silver that it seemed to be made of white fire. His moustache was like a spread of snowy wings.

The Royal Tea Taster strolled over to the line of women. He reached down into the first basket and picked out a sprig of tea. He held it up and looked at it very closely, frowning. He crushed the leaves and stuck his long nose into his cupped hands and sniffed a long, noisy sniff. Then he tossed the tea aside. He did this a few times along

the line, but more often he just glanced
into a basket and moved on. The Overseer
followed at a respectful distance, his hands
rubbing each other, his face wearing a sick
and frightened grin.

The Royal Tea Taster was quite close to
Sonam and Tashi when the Overseer lost
control of himself and dared to speak.

"Excellency, sir!" he said. "This tea, our
tea: it is very fine, is it not? Is it not a most
beautiful tea?"

The Royal Tea Taster lifted his nose as
if he had smelled a dead rat.

"Your tea," he said, "your tea is … ordinary."

The Overseer moaned and bent almost
double as if he had a great pain in his
stomach.

The Royal Tea Taster moved on and at last
stood before Sonam and Tashi. Tashi looked
up into his eyes, which were nearly as deep
and dark as the eyes of Rajah.

The Royal Tea Taster turned to walk away. Then he stopped. His nose twitched.

He came back to the basket that stood in front of Tashi and dipped his plump hand into it, testing the warm dampness of the leaves. He took a single sprig and studied it, twirling it between his fingers. He crushed it and sniffed it, twice.

"Where did you pick this?"

He spoke to Sonam, not to Tashi.

Sonam said, "Sir, I did not pick it. This child did. Her name is Tashi. She is the daughter of my sister, who is sick."

The Royal Tea Taster took a step back so that he could see Tashi over the gleaming bulge of his belly. His look was very stern. He lifted a hand and clicked his fingers.

The tiny sleeping man on the cart immediately woke up, jumped down and ran first to the back of the cart and then across to where the Royal Tea Taster stood. In one hand he carried a leather bag and in the other a small iron dish of burning charcoal, trailing smoke. He set the dish of charcoal on the ground and took from the bag a small copper kettle and a silver flask. He poured water from the flask into the kettle and sat the kettle on the fire and blew furiously onto the charcoal until it burned red.

The lid of the kettle rattled when the water boiled. The little man – who was in fact the Deputy Chief Tea Boiler – reached into the bag again and took out a milk-white porcelain bowl. It was so thin that Tashi could see the shadow of the little man's fingers through it. He put three sprigs of Tashi's tea into the bowl, poured boiling water onto them and handed the bowl to the Royal Tea Taster. The Royal Tea Taster held the bowl close to his nose and bent over. The little man then covered the Royal Tea Taster's head and the bowl with a white cloth. Tashi wanted to giggle but did not dare.

There was silence for several moments. Then from under the cloth there came a good deal of snuffling and sniffing: short shallow snuffles and some long deep sniffs and the kind of gasping that comes before a sneeze. Then another, longer silence. A hand came out from under the cloth. The fingers clicked again and the little man reached up and removed the cloth from the Royal Tea Taster's head.

When Tashi saw his face, the Royal Tea Taster no longer looked stern; he looked like a man who had seen an angel. He lifted the bowl to his lips and sucked in tea with a tremendous snorty slurping sound, which made Tashi jump. He rolled the tea around inside his mouth, first one cheek bulging, then the other. He opened his mouth slightly and drew in more air, gurgling. Then he turned his head and – *pfft!* – spat the tea onto the ground. Now he stood still with his eyes closed, breathing in and out through his mouth.

At last the Royal Tea Taster opened his eyes and sighed a sigh of pure joy. His smile was like the sun rising out of the mountains as he beamed down at Tashi.

"Come with me," he said.

He took her by the hand and together they walked over to the ox cart. The Royal Tea Taster studied the small anxious child who stood before him.

"In my life," he said, "I have tasted many, many kinds of tea. Perhaps a thousand kinds of tea. But until today I had tasted Cloud Tea only twice, and the last time was many years ago. And you know why, don't you?"

Tashi said nothing, because she could not think of anything to say.

"Of course you know. You know that Cloud Tea is almost impossible to find and even

more difficult to pick, because it grows up there." He pointed a finger up to where the mountains were wrapped in cloud. "It is the most magical and delicious tea in the world but it grows wild in high, dangerous places where men are afraid to go." He bent down to Tashi and spoke in a softer voice. "So I ask myself this: how could a small child have gathered this tea? Tell me, are you able to fly?"

Tashi lowered her eyes. Her tongue felt too big for her mouth. She knew that if she told this man the truth he would not believe her. She wondered if she was still asleep and dreaming.

"No, sir," she said. "I cannot fly."

"So. A small child cannot tell the Royal Tea Taster how she found the most valuable tea in the world. Is that correct?"

Tashi said, "Yes." It was the hardest word she'd ever had to say.

The Royal Tea Taster nodded seriously.
"Very well," he said. "I have my secrets
too." And then he smiled. "Come closer,"
he said, "and listen carefully. Exactly one
year from today I will come here again. And
I will come here again the year after that,
and every year after that. And each time I
come here I want you to bring me a basket
of Cloud Tea. And each time you bring me
a basket of Cloud Tea I will
give you one of these."

He held out a silk
pouch that was
small but heavy.
Tashi took it,
opened it and
looked inside.
The coins were fat
and made of gold,
and there were many
of them.

135

* * *

Just one of those fat gold coins was enough
to pay the doctor who came up from the
city to the tiny house on the mountain. The
cough that sounded like sticks breaking went
away and Tashi's mother grew strong again.
But she did not go back to the plantation to
work every day under the hot eye of the sun.

A year later, just one of those fat gold
coins was also enough to pay for fruit to fill
the tea basket: juicy mangoes, sleek bananas,
red-jewelled pomegranates, the rosiest
of apples, the most perfect of peaches.
In the shadow of the tree that grew from
the jumbled rocks, the monkeys feasted.

And afterwards, while Tashi dozed with
the babies on her lap, Rajah and the big
monkeys stole away up the mountains with
the empty basket and brought it back filled
with the magical green glow of Cloud Tea.

Later, the ox cart came; a plump hand

reached out of the purple shade and dropped a plump silk pouch into Tashi's palm.

There are only three people in the world who drink Cloud Tea. One of them is a little old woman who is called the Empress of All the Known World and Other Bits That Have Not Been Discovered Yet. The other two are a retired tea picker and her daughter, who live in a village among mountains whose tops are lost in clouds.

The Unforgotten Coat

FRANK COTTRELL BOYCE

Two refugee brothers from Mongolia are
determined to fit in with their Liverpool
schoolmates. However, they bring so much
of Mongolia to Bootle that their new friend
and guide, Julie, is hard-pressed to know truth
from fantasy. Told with the humour, warmth
and brilliance of detail which characterizes
Frank Cottrell Boyce's writing, this magical
and compelling story is enriched by stunning
and atmospheric Polaroid photos.

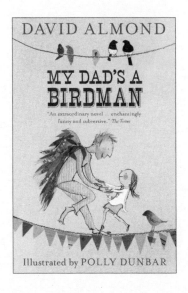

DAVID ALMOND

MY DAD'S A
BIRDMAN

"An extraordinary novel ... enchantingly
funny and subversive." *The Times*

Illustrated by POLLY DUNBAR

In a rainy town in the north of England, there are strange goings-on. **DAD** is building a pair of wings, eating flies and feathering his nest. **AUNTIE DOREEN** is getting cross and making dumplings. **MR POOP** is parading the streets shouting LOUDER and LOUDER, and even **MR MINT** the head teacher is getting in a flap. And watching it all is **LIZZIE**; missing her mam and looking after Dad and thinking how beautiful the birds are.

**"This original and touching tale
is an affirmation of love, trust and hope."**
The Sunday Times

The Kites Are Flying

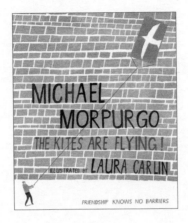

A television reporter's experience in the West Bank reveals how children's hopes and dreams for peace can fly higher than any wall dividing communities and religions.

"A wondrous tale of tragedy and hope."
Angels & Urchins

"Insightful and beautifully illustrated."
Daily Express